Stick & FETCH INVESTIGATE

A girl. A dog. A detective agency.

First published 2018 by Walker Books Ltd
87 Vauxhall Walk, London SE11 5HJ

10 9 8 7 6 5 4 3 2 1

British Library Cataloguing in Publication Data: a catalogue record for this book is available from the British Library

ISBN 978-1-4063-7644-9

www.walker.co.uk

MIX
Paper
FSC FSC® C101537

Stick & FETCH INVESTIGATE

BARKING UP THE WRONG TREE

Philip Ardagh

illustrated by

Elissa Elwick

WALKER
BOOKS

Meet Sally Stick and her dog
(and best friend), Fetch.

Together, they're:
STICK & FETCH, DETECTIVES.

Like most famous **DETECTIVES**, Stick and Fetch have their own special motto:

TRUST NO ONE, BELIEVE <u>EVERYTHING</u>

Or it could be:

TRUST EVERYTHING, BELIEVE <u>NO ONE</u>

To be honest, it might even be:

<u>TRUST NO ONE, DON'T BELIEVE ANYTHING</u>

Sally got the idea for a motto from something she was watching on TV. She quickly wrote it down on a paper napkin with a crayon, and it ended up looking like this:

After that, she and Fetch decided to leave their STICK & FETCH business cards blank.

"We can say it's a mystery why they're blank, like the mysteries we solve," Sally told Fetch.

"But don't **DETECTIVES** solve cases, not mysteries?" asked Fetch, sniffing an interesting corner of Granny Stick's fridge. (They live at Granny Stick's.)

Sally thought for a moment. "STICK & FETCH solve MYSTERIOUS cases," she announced.

Fetch was impressed. He wagged his tail.

Fetch isn't one of those fancy breeds of dog. He's a bit of a mixture.

But he's SALLY'S dog, so as far as Fetch is concerned, that makes him the BEST kind of dog there is.

And now he and Sally are detectives.

TELLY TROUBLE

One afternoon after school, the phone rang in the detective office of **STICK & FETCH**. They had hoped it would RING. They had wanted it to RING. But now that it had started to RING it was like a pin popping a balloon. The girl and dog both sat bolt upright in surprise.

RING
RING

The phone is rather an old-fashioned one attached to the wall. It is white, which Fetch rather likes because it makes it look even more like a bone. (Lots of things remind Fetch of bones.)

Sally once asked her granny if they could paint the phone red. (Important telephones are nearly always red.) But Granny Stick said no, and because the **STICK & FETCH** office is also her kitchen, Granny makes the rules.

Sally got up from her detective office desk (which is also the kitchen table) and hurried to answer the phone.

"**STICK & FETCH**," she said in her very best telephone manner. (This is the sort of voice she plans to use if she ever runs into a member of the Royal Family when out shopping.)

"This is Mrs Plink," said the voice at the other end. It sounded like a woman with a mouthful of marbles. "Please tell your granny that I'm about to explode—"

"Wh-what?" Sally gasped.

She dropped the phone, then

quickly snatched it up again.

"Hello? Hello?" she said, but there was no one there.

"Who was it?" barked Fetch.

"Someone called Mrs Plink..."

"Sounds like a made-up name to me," woofed Fetch. "I bet she has something to hide."

"Good thinking, Fetch."

"What did she want?"

"She said that she was about to explode."

"On purpose?" asked Fetch.

"I doubt it," said Sally. "No one explodes on purpose."

"Perhaps she's started blowing up like a balloon and can't stop!" said Fetch. "Maybe she'll blow up bigger and bigger, ROUNDER and ROUNDER, until she bursts!"

"That would be quite an explosion!" said Sally. "We must use our **DETECTIVE** powers to track her down. We must save her!" She leapt to her feet.

"But *how* will we save her?" asked Fetch.

"Let's worry about that once we've traced her," Sally suggested.

"Traced?" said Fetch, puzzled. "Like tracing the outline of a picture?"

"Trace is **DETECTIVE**-speak for 'find'," Sally reminded him. She has done a LOT of research about being a detective. "Like tracing a missing relative."

"Of course," said Fetch. "I knew that."

"Our first problem is that we don't know
where this Mrs Plink was calling from,"
said Sally. She put her hands behind
her back and paced up and down past
the fridge.

Fetch thought this looked very
detective-y, so he followed her
on all fours.

"Any **CLUES**?" he asked. **CLUES** are very important to detectives. **CLUES** are how they find things out. "Any noises in the background?"

"Yes!" said Sally. "Yes, there were! I could hear Tilly Dungwot off the telly."

"The newsreader with the funny haircut?"

"Yes," said Sally Stick. "*That* Tilly Dungwot."

Fetch wagged his tail excitedly.

"Then Mrs Plink must be at the TV studio!" he said. "It's the only explanation."

"You're right," said Sally. "You're so clever I could kiss you!" And she did, because, although detectives don't usually kiss each other, Fetch is her dog, remember. "Let's go!"

A few minutes later, Sally was pedalling her bicycle frantically, peering around Fetch, who'd taken up his usual position in the basket in front.

Stick and Fetch looked a bit like a
large bush riding a bike with a basketful
of candyfloss, at least to their elderly

neighbour, Mrs Mason, watching them from her window without her glasses on.

It didn't take the pair too long to reach the TV studio. Sally only made a couple of wrong turns, and Fetch only jumped out of the basket once, when his arch-nemesis,* a Persian cat called Tofu, taunted him from the top of a traffic light.

*worst enemy

At the studio, Sally chained her bike to the railings then walked up to the security guard at the gate.

"Hello," said Sally.

The security guard was looking down at Fetch.

"Do you like my dog?" asked Sally.

"I am very handsome," Fetch pointed out. All the security guard could hear, however, was **WOOF! WOOF! WOOF!** because that's all *anyone* can hear when Fetch speaks. Except for Sally, of course. She understands everything he says. This is one of the reasons why they make such a great team.

The security guard patted Fetch.

"What breed of dog is he?" he asked.

"I am a very rare breed," barked Fetch.
"Tell him, Sally."

"He's a mixture," said Stick.

"See?" said Fetch proudly. "How many other Mixtures have you met?"

"He *is* cute," said the guard.

"CUTE?" said Fetch in horror. "I think you mean HANDSOME." Of course, all the man heard was **WOOF! WOOF! WOOF!**

"We're here to be on the news," said Sally.

"Then you must be on my list," said the guard. He peered at his clipboard. "The lady sumo wrestler has already gone in, so you can't be her..."

Sally had no idea what a lady sumo wrestler was.

"That just leaves Mr Jones," said the security guard. He looked down at Sally then up at his list again and frowned. "You can't be Mr Jones," he said.

Sally laughed.
"Of course I'm not!"
"I didn't think so."
The guard smiled.
"*He* is," said Sally.
She pointed at Fetch.

A detective has to be good at thinking on her feet. (She has to be good at thinking on her bottom, too, if she's sitting down.) She has to be quick at coming up with ideas on the spot.

"*He's* Mr Jones?" said the security guard, somewhat puzzled.

"Not really," Fetch confessed. **WOOF**.

"He is," said Sally in her special no-nonsense voice.

"I wonder why your name isn't on the list too?" said the security guard. He studied his clipboard again.

"I guess I'm not important enough," said Sally. "After all, Mr Jones here is the star. But he can't travel alone — being a dog."

"Fair enough," said the guard, opening the gate. "In you go."

TV STUDIO

Lady Sumo Wrestler ☑

Mr Jones ☑

Frog Expert ☑

**ALL VISITORS MUST
REPORT TO RECEPTION.**

Sally didn't like tricking the nice man,
but she was a detective on a case with
no time to lose. Mrs Plink might explode at
any minute!

Stick and Fetch walked up to a large,
shoebox-shaped building with two doors.
There was a sign on each.

AUTHORIZED PERSONNEL ONLY

Badges must be worn
at all times.

"What are **AUTHORIZED PERSONNEL?**"
asked Fetch, who is very good at reading
for a dog.

"I don't know," said Sally. "But you need a badge." Sally was already wearing one. It was from the library and had a picture of a book on it. (She and Granny Stick go to the library together most Saturdays.)

"No one will know if I'm wearing a badge or not under all my fur," woofed Fetch.

"Good thinking!" Sally smiled. She buried her fingers in the fur on top of his head and gave him a good old rub. (Fetch doesn't let anyone else do that. Just his Sally.) If he'd been a cat he would have purrrrrred.

The first thing the detective duo noticed was that it was hard to notice anything because it was so very dark.

They walked around a bit until they came to a brightly lit area with people bustling around the unlit edges. In the middle was the news desk.

"There's Tilly Dungwot," whispered Sally.

Fetch didn't answer her because dogs can't whisper very well.

Sitting next to Miss Dungwot was a very large person. A super-large person. An enormously ROUND person. A person round enough to explode without warning...

"That must be Mrs Plink!" gasped Sally.

"What shall we do?" said Fetch in his lowest possible growl.

Several important-looking people
turned and **shushed** them.

Shush! Shush! **SHUSH!**

Sally headed for a shadowy corner and
Fetch skidded after her, claws clattering
on the highly polished floor.

"We could try popping her," Sally
hissed.

"Won't that hurt?" woofed Fetch.

"Not as much as swelling and swelling
until she *EXPLODES*!" said Sally.

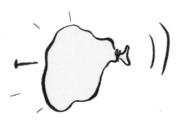

"Then let's do it!" said Fetch. "I'll give her a prod with a carefully chosen claw."

"Good luck, **_DETECTIVE_**!" said Stick.

"Thank you, **_DETECTIVE_**," said Fetch.

Tilly Dungwot was asking the very large lady a question about sumo wrestling ...

... when Fetch bounded over and jabbed the lady in the bottom with a claw. With a roar like an injured elephant, the lady leapt into the air ...

TV STUDIO

... and landed ...

... on top ...

... of Tilly Dungwot.

The newsreader and the sumo wrestler both went crashing to the studio floor.

Fetch was now back at Sally's side, panting with excitement.

"Good work!" Sally said. "You saved her from blowing to bits. She'll soon be back to her original size. Our work here is done." She pushed her hair out of her eyes. "Come on, Fetch."

Together, girl and dog walked calmly
out of the studio, ignored by everyone
rushing to help the two women: one **fat**
and one **f-l-a-t**.

The detective duo strolled past the security guard, who seemed to be having an argument with a man in a horrid suit.

"Bye!" Sally called out, with a wave.

WOOF! said Fetch. (Well, what he actually said was, "Goodbye!", but what everyone but Sally heard was **WOOF!**)

When Stick and Fetch arrived home, they found Granny Stick sitting at the kitchen table drinking tea with a stranger. The stranger was a tall, thin lady with a nose like a parrot's beak. She was grinning and almost BOUNCING in her chair.

"Hello!" said Sally. "I'm Sally and this is Fetch." She pointed at her fellow detective.

"This is Mrs Plink," said Granny Stick. "She's very excited."

"**EXPLODING** with excitement!" agreed Mrs Plink. She sounded as if she had a mouthful of marbles. "Your granny and I just had recipes published in the local paper!"

"We're having cake to celebrate," said Granny Stick. "There's enough for all of us."

But Sally was only half listening. *Plink*, she thought. *Now where have I heard that name before?*

"Who's she?" Fetch asked his best friend and detective partner.

"No idea," said Sally.

The phone rang.

"Would you answer that, please, Sally?" asked Granny Stick.

"Sure," said Sally. "This could be another case for STICK & FETCH."

NO
CLOWNING
AROUND

One Saturday, Sally and Fetch came back from shadowing Tofu to find an empty picture frame on the desk in the office of **STICK & FETCH** (also known as the kitchen table). Tofu, you may remember, is Fetch's arch-nemesis — worst enemy — and shadowing means "following someone without them knowing".

Stick and Fetch had
been good at the "following"
part – until Tofu had dashed up
a tree. He had then glared at
them with a "Stop following me!"
look, which suggested that
they weren't so good at the
"without them knowing"
part.

"Look!" said Sally, now holding up the empty frame.

"What use is a picture frame without a picture in it?" asked Fetch, thinking like the detective that he was.

"Actually, I **DEDUCE** it's a *photo* frame without a *photo* in it," said Sally. **DEDUCE** is a detective word meaning "work out". (In other words, it's more than just a guess.)

Fetch was impressed. He wagged his tail. "Good work, **DETECTIVE**," he woofed.

"How can you tell?"

"Because of the writing on this back bit, which comes off," Sally explained.

"PHOTO FRAME," Fetch read aloud, being a good reader (for a dog).

"And what good is a photo frame without a photo in it?" asked Sally.

"No good at all," said Fetch.

"Hmm," Sally said. "Are you thinking what I'm thinking?"

"You don't mean...?" began Fetch.

"I do mean." Sally nodded. "I think that this photo frame *had* a photo in it ..."

"... and that someone has STOLEN it?" said Fetch. He ran around the kitchen floor in circles.

"EXACTLY," said Sally. "I think the owner of the stolen photo has left this on our desk because they want us to find it for them!"

For a long time now, STICK & FETCH, DETECTIVES had been hoping to solve a big art robbery. At last, here was their chance! It wasn't a billion-pound painting, but it was a start.

"See any **CLUES**?" woofed Fetch.

"Well, there *is* this," said Sally, picking up a piece of paper from the floor. "It looks like the torn-off corner of a newspaper."

She gave Fetch a closer look. He sniffed it.

"It *smells* like the torn-off corner of a newspaper," he announced.

"So we can safely **DEDUCE*** that it IS the torn-off corner of a newspaper," said Sally triumphantly. "I bet it was dropped by the photo thief."

She studied the scrap of newspaper more closely. "Look!" she said. "A few squares of a crossword. And it's been filled in with GREEN ink!"

*That word again!   59

She waved the paper in front of Fetch's nose a second time. He breathed in deeply. "It does smell inky and GREEN!" he admitted. **WOOF! WOOF!**

"So where should we begin our **investigation**?" Sally wondered.

Their eyes met. "At Pete's Paper Shop!" they said, as one.

Pete's Paper Shop is the name of the paper shop owned by Pete. It sells newspapers, magazines and greetings cards (and sweets, of course).

"Let's get down there," said Sally. "Maybe we'll find the photo!"

They dashed out of the kitchen door to her bike, and Fetch jumped into the basket on the front. "To the paper shop!" he barked.

Pete's Paper Shop is where Sally and Fetch go to collect Granny Stick's paper every morning. They both like Pete very much. And he likes them. He once gave Sally a whole pile of old magazines to use for an art project.

"Hello, Sally! Hello, Fetch!" Pete called out as they entered his shop.

"Hello!" Fetch replied. All Pete heard was a **WOOF!** but that was good enough for him.

"Hello, Mr Pete. Do any of your customers do the crossword in green ink?" Sally asked, getting straight down to business.

"A lot of people who come in here like a good crossword," said Pete, "but I've no idea what colour ink they use." He paused.

"What is it?" asked Sally.

"Well, it's funny you should ask me about green ink. I just put a postcard in the window for someone, and I thought it was unusual that he'd written it in green."

"Which postcard, Pete?" Fetch asked.

WOOF! WOOF!

"Fetch asked which one," said Sally, translating.

"The one written in green ink, of course," said the newsagent with a smile.

"Of course," said Fetch, looking down at

his front paws. (I would say "sheepishly", but he looks pretty sheep-like much of the time anyway, what with all that fur.)

WOOF! he said. "I knew that."

Stick and Fetch hurried back out onto the pavement to look in the shop window. There were a number of handwritten postcards on display. They advertised everything from spare rooms to gardening services.

There was only one written in green:

CHUCKLES THE CLOWN:
MAGIC AND MAYHEM!

"That handwriting is nothing like
the letters in the crossword," Fetch
commented.

"He probably *disguises* his handwriting,
being a photo thief and that," said Sally.

Fetch agreed. "Also, being a clown
is a perfect *disguise*," he barked. "You
can't see what someone really looks like

under their clown wig, clown nose and
clown make-up!"

"I bet his name isn't even Chuckles," said Sally. "I bet it's an *alias*."

"An alien?" Fetch gasped. "You think Chuckles the Clown is from Outer Space?"

"Not an *alien*, silly," said Stick. "I said an *alias*. An *alias* is a false name." (She'd read that in the **BIG BOOK OF DETECTIVE TALES** that Granny Stick had given her for her last birthday.) "I don't think Chuckles is our thief's real name."

"So, photo-stealing Chuckles has a made-up name, a made-up clown face and made-up handwriting!" said Fetch. "**WOW!**" (It was a very woofy "Wow!")

"And there he is!" Sally gasped. She pointed to a man who'd just appeared on the other side of the road. He looked nothing like a clown.

Fetch wondered how she knew it was Chuckles. He decided to apply his own detective skills.

He spotted that:

🔍 The man was carrying a large patchwork bag. Poking out of the top were an inflatable pink flamingo, an inflatable banana and an inflatable hammer.

🔍 The man had a green pen sticking out of his top pocket.

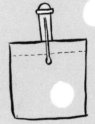

The man had a car key in his hand and was climbing into the driving seat of a van with CHUCKLES THE CLOWN: MAGIC AND MAYHEM! written on the side.

Hmm. All good clues, especially that last one. Fetch jumped back into the basket of Sally's bike. "Let's get after him!" he woofed.

Five minutes later, Sally Stick was pedalling frantically up the crunchy gravel drive of Poshington Hall, the local manor house. (Sally had been to a party there once.)

By the time Stick and Fetch reached
the house, Chuckles had already parked
his van and was heading up the front
steps with his bagful of props. He
disappeared through the large front door.

Various children were getting out of various cars, each carrying a present.

Stick and Fetch ducked behind the clown's van.

"It looks like Chuckles is performing at a children's birthday party," woofed Fetch out of the corner of his mouth.

"And it looks like *that's* the birthday boy," said Sally.

"Nice **DETECTIVE** work, Stick!" said Fetch.

"Thank you, Fetch," said Sally.

Standing beside the birthday boy was a tall, grey-haired man dressed in a chauffeur's uniform. Neither of them

looked very happy. Truth be told,
they both looked a bit gloomy.

Sally was about to stand up from her hiding place when she sensed that she was being watched. She turned to find a little boy looking at her intently. He had a present tucked under one arm and a finger up one nostril.

"What are you doing?" he asked.

"I can't tell you," Sally whispered.
"We're working on a case. We're **DETECTIVES**."

"You *and* your dog?"

"Yes," said Sally.

The boy's eyes were wide with excitement. "COOL!" he said, then turned and ran away.

"Come on," Sally said to Fetch. "If it's a kids' party, it should be easy enough to get in. I'm a kid."

"True," woofed Fetch. "But what if someone recognizes you as the great **DETECTIVE**? And you haven't brought a present. Everyone else has a present."

"You have a point. Two points, in fact," said Sally. "I'll kneel. That'll make me smaller than me so they won't know it *is* me. And you can be my present."

"Excellent thinking!" Fetch wagged his tail and nodded his head at the same time. From a distance, he looked as though he was wagging at both ends.

The detectives waited until all the guests had gone inside, then skedaddled across the gravel driveway and up the steps.

At the door, Sally took off her shoes, knelt down and slid them under her knees so they looked like her feet at the end of a much shorter pair of legs.

"What should I do to look present-like?" asked Fetch as they entered a large hallway. It smelt strongly of polish, and everything there looked very expensive but a bit old.

Sally spotted a metal stand with a handwritten sign at the top, directing the guests to the party.* Tethered to the sign by a thin blue string was a helium **HAPPY BIRTHDAY** balloon.

Sally quickly stood up, untied the string and attached the balloon to Fetch's collar. She then knelt back down on her shoes.

"Try and look like a toy dog," Sally whispered.

---

*The sign wasn't really necessary — anyone could have followed the excited squeals of the children.

Fetch scratched the back of his head with a paw. He wasn't convinced. "How do I do that?" he asked.

"Imagine you've got batteries inside you," Sally suggested.

The pair made their way across the floor, Sally Stick walking awkwardly on her knees and Fetch trying to move as stiffly as a battery-powered pooch.

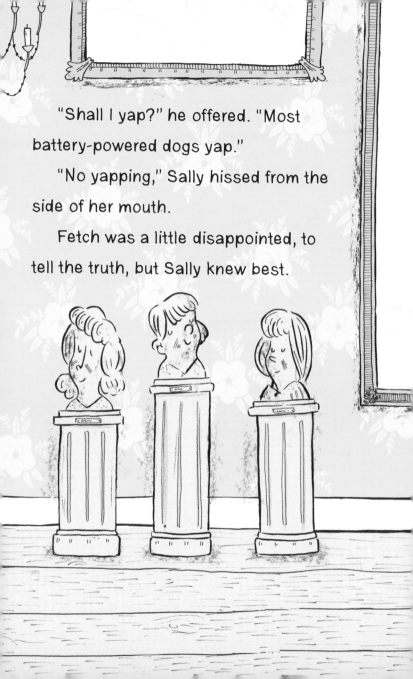

"Shall I yap?" he offered. "Most battery-powered dogs yap."

"No yapping," Sally hissed from the side of her mouth.

Fetch was a little disappointed, to tell the truth, but Sally knew best.

No one took any notice of the detective duo as they entered the party room. All eyes were on Chuckles the Clown who had, just that minute, appeared from behind a screen.

There were claps and cheers and whoops from the children sitting on the floor and their parents in the seats. Fetch noticed that Birthday Boy Edward still looked far from happy.

"What now?" he asked

Sally in his quietest woof.

"We keep our **DETECTIVE** eyes out for
stolen photographs," said Sally.

To be honest, Sally and Fetch enjoyed
watching the show. Chuckles made a very
good clown, and there was a mixture of
laughs and party magic, from a seemingly
endless stream of coloured hankies to
magic wands that drooped like wilting
flowers.

Then things got serious. "Look what
I've got here, boys and girls!" said

Chuckles, picking up a great big thick book. "It's a photo album. Full of photos!"

Photo album? A look passed between Stick and Fetch. A professional-detective look.

Chuckles opened the album to show the audience that it was, indeed, full of colourful photographs. "But, if I tweak my magic nose three times –" which he did, *squeak, squeak, squeak!* – "the photos disappear!" He flipped through the album again, and all the photos had ...

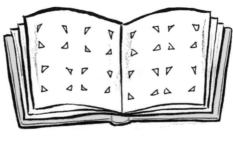

... GONE!

"Thief!" shouted Fetch, unable to hold back any longer – though of course everyone but Sally heard it as **WOOF!** – and then a huge ball of tangled fur was throwing itself at the clown.

Chuckles went tumbling over onto his back, landing with his great big clown feet in the air. Birthday Boy Edward smiled a small smile, which quickly turned into a BIG smile, followed by an explosion of laughter.

Other children shrieked. There were shouts and cries and general confusion.

Fetch, meanwhile, sat on the clown's chest, waiting for reinforcements.

These arrived, moments later, in the form of Sally, who'd lost her shoes along the way. She bent over, grabbed the album and said, "No more stealing photographs. We're on to you!"

A small boy with his finger up his nose
turned solemnly to a baby in a pushchair
next to him. "They're **DETECTIVES**, you
know," he said. "Working a case."

The baby gurgled with interest.

Before anyone quite knew what was
happening, Fetch and Sally Stick, album in
hand, had dashed out of the room.

"Doggy!" cried a small voice.

The detectives heard the sound of
large shoes slapping down on the wooden
floor somewhere behind them. Chuckles
was in hot pursuit and the audience
wasn't far behind.

Birthday Boy Edward was now whoop-whoop-whooping — that's TRIPLE whooping — in delight.

Fetch's claws skittered across the polished floors like the patter of raindrops, and he and Sally dashed and ducked and dived, running through doorways and down corridors.

"Quick, in here!" Fetch barked,

skidding to a halt and diving into a big
vase.

Sally clambered into the even bigger
vase next to it. The balloon slipped free
from Fetch's collar and floated up to the
ceiling, bobbing safely out of sight. Down
below, Stick and Fetch ducked from view.

Just in time!

They heard the clown charging past
moments later, followed by the laughing
children. Then there was quiet for a while.
Then the children went round again. Then
there was quiet. And then... (You get the
idea.) Until, at last, silence.

Who knows how long they stayed

there, but Sally's whole body was beginning to ache and she was worried that Granny Stick would be expecting them home for tea.

Then Sally and Fetch heard two sets of footsteps walk towards them.

Fetch sniffed the air. Cake. He poked his head out of his vase. There, standing right beside him, was Birthday Boy Edward and the grey-haired chauffeur. They were both grinning.

The chauffeur politely knocked on Sally's vase. She stuck her head out.

"The others have gone, madam," he said. "The coast, as they say, is clear."

"Oh," said Sally. "Good."

"I like your dog," said Edward, patting
Fetch. "He's brilliant."

"I am, rather, aren't I?" said
Fetch. **WOOF! WOOF!**

"I'm Stick and he's my partner, Fetch,"
Sally told the boy. "We're **STICK & FETCH**,
famous **DETECTIVES**. You've probably
heard of us." She fumbled in her pocket
and handed him a slightly crumpled card.
"Our business card," she said.

"Amazing!" said Edward. He looked at
the card and turned it over. It was blank on
both sides. "We saved you some cake."

"Cake?" asked Fetch, eyeing the
generous slice of birthday cake sitting

on a paper plate in the chauffeur's hand.
WOOF!

In a single move, Fetch managed to jump out of the vase and snaffle the piece of cake. The whole thing would have been more impressive if he hadn't ended up with so many crumbs in his fur.

"Manners!" said Stick.

"Sorry!" said Fetch.

Sally turned to Edward. "Thank you! And Happy Birthday!"

"Yes, Happy Birthday!" Fetch woofed.

"From Fetch too," said Sally.

"Are you on a case?" asked Edward.

"Yes. And it's **solved**," said Sally, who was discovering that it was much harder to get out of a vase than to jump into one.

The chauffeur gave her a helping hand. "I don't think the culprit will be in such a hurry to steal any more photos now that he knows we're on to him."

"I don't understand, Miss Stick," said the chauffeur.

"I'm sorry, but we don't discuss cases," said Sally.

"*Sorry?* This is my best birthday ever!" said Edward. And that was quite something, what with his mum in hospital and his dad away.

"We were just doing our job," said Fetch modestly. (All good detectives should be brilliant AND modest.)

WOOF!
WOOF!
WOOF!

"Good day!" said Sally. "Duty calls!"
(Whatever that meant.)

"You'll need these," said the chauffeur,
handing her her shoes.

Back home, one bike ride later, Stick and
Fetch found Granny Stick hammering a
nail into the kitchen wall.

"Hello, you two!" she said. She put
down the hammer and proceeded to hang
up a photograph of all three of them at the
Summer Show. The frame looked familiar.

"Mrs Mason's son printed out this photo on his new printer," she said, referring to their neighbour. "Wasn't that kind of him?"

"Very," said Sally. A lot seemed to be happening with photos that day.

Granny Stick sat down at the kitchen table, put on her glasses and pulled a puzzle book and pen out of her enormous handbag. She took the green cap off the green pen. "So, what have you two been up to today?" she asked.

"Fighting crime," said Fetch. "Fighting crime."

But of course all Granny Stick could hear was **WOOF. WOOF. WOOF.**

UP,

UP

AND

AWAY

There's something strange in the garden," said Fetch, one soggy day. He had his front paws resting on the ledge of the kitchen window as he peered out.

"Where?" asked Sally Stick, hurrying to his side. "Do you think we're being **spied** on?" It was the first week of the Christmas holidays, and it was about time they had a new case to solve.

"We could be," said Fetch. "When you've solved as many cases as we have, you make enemies in the criminal underpants."

"Under*world*," Sally corrected him. Although Fetch has an amazing vocabulary for a dog, he does sometimes get his words mixed up.

"Oh," said Fetch. "There it is again!" he woofed, pressing his nose to the glass.

Sally saw it too. Something yellow bobbing behind the bare winter branches of a bush. (It was far too cold for leaves, so they'd sensibly fallen off months before.) Was it a head ducking out of sight? No, it was ...

"A balloon!" they both said at once.

WOOF!

Despite the rain, the pair dashed out into the garden.

Sally Stick lifted the balloon from the bush, where it had become entangled.

"Careful!" said Fetch. They didn't want it to pop. (They're both big fans of balloons.)

They studied it. The balloon was yellow with red writing on it:

"Wow!" said Fetch.

"Wow," agreed Sally. "An eighty-year-old balloon!"

"That's amazing," said Fetch, giving it a really good sniff. "This balloon is even older than Granny Stick!"

"What's it doing in our back garden?" said Sally.

80

YEARS OLD TO

"And where do you think it's come from?" asked Fetch.

"An eighty-year-old balloon must be rare," Sally pointed out. "It's unlikely to have come from Pete's Paper Shop." She frowned her "I'm a detective doing some serious thinking" frown. "But it must belong somewhere. Where are most old, rare things kept?"

"The TOWN MUSEUM?" said Fetch. He began to pant, which is what he does when he gets excited.

"Precisely." Sally nodded.

"So what's it doing here?" said her dog.

Both Sally's hair and Fetch's fur were beginning to get a little soggy in the rain, so they headed back inside with their find.

"You know what I think?" said Sally, wiping her feet on the doormat. "I think someone must have broken into the museum and stolen this very rare, very old balloon, then dropped it while making their getaway."

"But why did they come through our back garden?"

"They didn't, or you would have sniffed out their tracks," said Sally. "I suspect the balloon floated here once the thief dropped it."

"Good work, **DETECTIVE**!" woofed Fetch.

He waited on the mat while Sally wiped each of his paws in turn with a piece of paper towel. Granny Stick likes to keep the kitchen floor nice and clean.

"Do you think we should take it back to the museum?"

"Not yet," said Sally. "First we should

go to the museum and find out if anything else has gone missing."

"You mean...?"

"Yes," said Sally. "This is another case for STICK & FETCH."

They arrived at the TOWN MUSEUM to find it closed.

"But the museum is NEVER closed," said Fetch.

"Except at night and on Sundays and on Christmas Day," Sally reminded him. It's important to be accurate with the facts when you're a detective.

"And today certainly isn't Christmas Day," Fetch agreed.

"Or night, or a Sunday!" said Sally with growing excitement. "But if there's been a robbery, they'd probably have to close the museum while the police investigate."

"So our hump was right!" woofed Fetch.

"You mean **hunch**," Sally corrected him kindly. "Something based on a feeling is a **hunch**, not a *hump*."

Fetch stored away the information in his doggy brain.

Both Stick and Fetch like the museum and the lady who runs it. The museum lady's title is TOWN MUSEUM CURATOR, and her name is Ms Finch. Fetch likes her because she smells of

Marmite. Sally Stick likes her because she doesn't mind dogs in the museum (as long as they behave).

It didn't look like they would be getting inside today, though.

"There's not so much as a catflap open, by the looks of it," said Sally.

At the mention of the word "cat", Fetch looked around to make sure that Tofu, his Persian-cat arch-nemesis, was nowhere to be seen. Not a whisker.

"Let's go and have a look around the outside," said Sally, rather wishing her coat had a hood, and off they went.

They came to a large window that looked into one of the ground-floor galleries, which was made to look like a grand Victorian dining room with a table laid as if for a big dinner.

The sight of all that pretend food made Fetch's stomach rumble through his fur.

"Sorry," he said. "My tummy's not very good at telling pretend food from the real thing."

"No sign of anyone," said Sally, but then she saw something that made

her eyes widen. "Wait! Look above the fireplace!" she cried.

Fetch looked. "There's nothing there."

WOOF.

"*Exactly,*" said Sally Stick. "But remember what we talked about?"

Fetch thought VERY hard (not that you could see his thinking frown). "I know!" he barked excitedly. "Sometimes what's NOT there is as important as what is. Like a library without books or a buggy without a baby!"

"Precisely!" said Sally. (She got the expression from watching one of Granny's favourite American cop shows.) "And there

must have been something above the
fireplace, but it's not there any more. See?
There's a dark square on the wallpaper

where there must have been a picture or a mirror."

"You don't think...?"

"I DO think!" said Sally. "I think that whoever stole the eighty-year-old balloon stole something off this wall, too."

Fetch jumped down from his flowerpot when something caught his eye. "Look!" he said. "It could be a *CLUE*!"

It was an old gardening glove.

"Good work, Fetch!" said Sally giving him a hug. "That's definitely a *CLUE*.

Thieves wear gloves. So now we know that our thief is a one-armed thief!"

"We do?"

"We do. Thieves wear gloves so they don't leave any fingerprints. There'd be no point in wearing just one—"

"Of course! Unless they only have one arm," said Fetch. He was so excited that he rolled in a patch of mud, then instantly felt embarrassed. Professional detectives do NOT roll in the mud. He gave the glove a sniff. "I smell flowers," he said.

"Any particular type of flower?" asked Sally. "This could be important."

"Could it?" asked Fetch.

"Yes, it could. Say, for example, the flower is honeysuckle and we find a one-armed man who HATES honeysuckle, then we can rule him out of our **investigation**."

Fetch couldn't hide how impressed he was with his fellow detective. He gave her a huge lick. Then he sniffed the glove again.

"Let's go somewhere where there are lots of flowers," said Sally. "That way, you can smell them and try to match them to the flowers on the glove."

"The park?" suggested Fetch.

"No, not the park," said Sally. "It's the wrong time of year." She hurried back towards her bike. "Let's go!"

"Where?"

"You'll see!"

Soon they were cycling frantically into town.

There is only one florist in their town: Strictly Floral. Stick and Fetch had

128

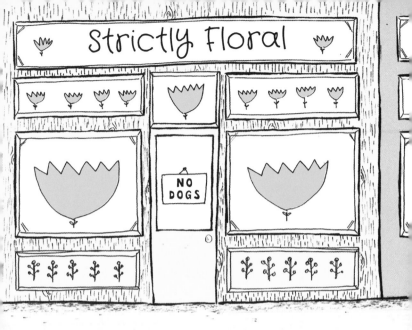

passed it many times, but they had never
been inside. This was their destination.

"Oh," said Sally when they pulled up
outside. Her face dropped. "We have a
problem." She pointed at a **NO DOGS** sign.

"Hmm," woofed Fetch, whose reading, you may remember, is excellent. "How can I smell the different flowers if I can't even get inside the shop?" He threw himself flat on the pavement and stuck his snout right up against the crack at the bottom of the door. He breathed in an overpowering scent of all kinds of flowers.

It made him feel **WOOZY**. "Smell
overload!" he shouted in panic.

But Sally Stick's attention was
suddenly elsewhere. "Fetch!" she said
urgently. "Get up!"

"What is it?" said Fetch.

"I just saw some pirates go into the library over the road!"

"Pirates?"

"One has a wooden leg and another has a hook instead of a hand ..."

"... AND A ONE-HANDED THIEF ONLY NEEDS ONE GLOVE!" barked Fetch with such excitement that it caused a passing lady to drop a pork pie in surprise.

"So it wasn't a one-*armed* man we were looking for, but a one-*handed* man!" said Sally Stick triumphantly.

"*If* that's our balloon thief," said Fetch.

"Of course it's our balloon thief!" said Sally. "Pirates steal stuff. It's their job."

"You're right!" said Fetch.

"Then let's go!" said Sally.

Mr Bennett, the librarian, didn't notice that Fetch had sneaked into the library with Sally because he was too busy supervising Story Time.

Three pirates sat facing the children, surrounded by balloons. One of them had a book open on his knee. It was called PATCHY THE PIRATE'S BIG ADVENTURE. On the wall behind the pirates hung what looked like an oil painting of a pirate with a menacing grin and a great big beard.

 Sally looked at the painting and thought of the blank spot on the museum wall.

She looked at the pirates in front of the painting, particularly the one with a plastic hook where his right hand should be. She thought of the single glove the thief had dropped.

She looked at all the balloons and thought of the balloon they'd found in the back garden.

And, finally, she looked at a big vase of flowers on the windowsill. The glove had smelt of flowers.

"We've found our balloon thief all right!" she whispered.

"What shall we do?" growled Fetch.

"ARREST HIM!" shouted Sally, bounding forwards.

What happened next was a bit of a blur. Later, children talked about a big ball of fur that seemed to come out of nowhere. They talked about the one-legged pirate who ran so fast that she seemed to forget that she had one leg and instantly grew another. And about the girl who suddenly appeared, causing the oil-painting to fall on two of the pirates and ... and ... what an EXCITING Story Time!

A while later, a little soggy but very pleased, Sally and Fetch were back home again. Granny Stick was next door celebrating her neighbour Mrs Mason's eightieth birthday. Sally held up the plastic hook, which one of the pirates had somehow lost in the kerfuffle.

"I don't think HE'LL be committing any more crimes in a hurry!" she said. "Now all we need to do is return the balloon to the museum."

So, the very next day, they went to the TOWN MUSEUM. They arrived to find the door wide open and two workmen in overalls carrying a large mirror out of a van, up the steps and through the main entrance.

Unfortunately, the **80 YEARS OLD TODAY!** balloon had somehow burst on the way, so Sally Stick simply slid it under Ms Finch's office door.

"And now," she said, turning to Fetch, "we're ready to solve another case! Let's go."

"We're good at being **DETECTIVES**, aren't we?" said Fetch.

"We most certainly are," said Stick.

And off they went.

PHILIP ARDAGH has won lots of awards, mostly for writing. Not one is for detecting. He's never had a dog, but if he did, he'd want one just like Fetch. Philip does have a big bushy beard, though, and they go everywhere together.

ELISSA ELWICK writes as well as illustrates, but, like Philip, never quite got the knack of detecting. She grew up with dogs around the house and hopes to have a real-life Fetch of her own one day. (She already has the bicycle and the basket.)